D1168289

Dear Parent:
Your child's love of reading starts here!

Every child learns to read in a different way and at his or her own speed. Some go back and forth between reading levels and read favorite books again and again. Others read through each level in order. You can help your young reader improve and become more confident by encouraging his or her own interests and abilities. From books your child reads with you to the first books he or she reads alone, there are I Can Read Books for every stage of reading:

SHARED READING
Basic language, word repetition, and whimsical illustrations, ideal for sharing with your emergent reader

BEGINNING READING
Short sentences, familiar words, and simple concepts for children eager to read on their own

READING WITH HELP
Engaging stories, longer sentences, and language play for developing readers

READING ALONE
Complex plots, challenging vocabulary, and high-interest topics for the independent reader

ADVANCED READING
Short paragraphs, chapters, and exciting themes for the perfect bridge to chapter books

I Can Read Books have introduced children to the joy of reading since 1957. Featuring award-winning authors and illustrators and a fabulous cast of beloved characters, I Can Read Books set the standard for beginning readers.

A lifetime of discovery begins with the magical words "I Can Read!"

Visit www.icanread.com for information
on enriching your child's reading experience.

I Can Read Book® is a trademark of HarperCollins Publishers.

The Berenstain Bears Are SuperBears! Copyright © 2015 by Berenstain Publishing, Inc. All rights reserved. Manufactured in China. No part of this book may be used or reproduced in any manner whatsoever without written permission except in the case of brief quotations embodied in critical articles and reviews. For information address HarperCollins Children's Books, a division of HarperCollins Publishers, 195 Broadway, New York, NY 10007.
www.icanread.com

Library of Congress Control Number: 2014960371
ISBN 978-0-06-235009-1 (trade bdg.) —ISBN 978-0-06-235008-4 (pbk.)

15 16 17 18 19 SCP   10 9 8 7 6 5 4 3 2 1   ❖   First Edition

I Can Read!

BEGINNING
1
READING

The Berenstain Bears®

Are SUPERBEARS!

Mike Berenstain

Based on the characters created by
Stan and Jan Berenstain

HARPER

An Imprint of HarperCollinsPublishers

Brother and Sister Bear liked to pretend they were SuperBears. Brother liked to be Bat Bear.

Sister liked to be Spider Bear.

Honey was their sidekick,

Cubby Bear.

The three SuperBears went outside.

They were looking for villains.

They saw the mailbear delivering the mail.

"Look!" said Brother.

"It is the evil Dr. Sleezo.

He is stealing the mail!"

The SuperBears jumped out.

"Halt, Dr. Sleezo!" they cried.

"We are SuperBears!

You must stop your evil ways!"

"Curses. Foiled again!" said the mailbear.

He delivered the mail and went away.

The SuperBears looked for more villains.

They saw a trash truck.

The workers were emptying trash cans.

"Look!" said Sister.

"Space Grizzlies are coming.

They are in their Grizz Ship.

They want to steal our superpods.

We need them for our superpowers!"

The SuperBears jumped out.

"Halt, Space Grizzlies!" they said.

"We are SuperBears!

Go back to your evil planet, Grizzlon!"

"Oh no!" said the workers, smiling.

"We must go back to Grizzlon now."

They emptied the trash and went away.

The SuperBears looked for more villains.

They saw a worker fixing the wires.

"Look!" said Brother.

"It is the mad villain Joker Bear.

He is trying to wreck the supernet!"

The SuperBears ran to the pole.

"Halt, Joker Bear!" they said.

"We are SuperBears!

You must stop your mad plot!"

"Oh well," said the worker, smiling.

"My mad plot will have to wait."

He went on fixing the wires.

The SuperBears were
having a fine day.

Then a young cub came by on his bike.

He hit a bump and fell off.

He hurt his knee.

The SuperBears wiped the cub's eyes.

They wiped his nose.

They helped him get back on his bike.

And then they helped him get home.

"My poor baby!" said the cub's mother.
"You three cubs really are SuperBears!"
She gave each SuperBear a big kiss.

The SuperBears waved good-bye.

Now they were getting hungry.

It was time to go to SuperBase for lunch.

Mama Bear fixed the SuperBears lunch.

They had peanut-butter-and-honey

sandwiches.

"Thank you, SuperMama!" they said.

"You're welcome, SuperBears," said Mama. "Now go out and fight those villains!"

The three SuperBears ran outside.

"On, SuperBears!" they cried.

"Villains beware!"